This igloo book belongs to:

....

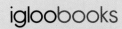

Published in 2016
by Igloo Books Ltd
Cottage Farm
Sywell
NN6 0BJ
www.igloobooks.com

HUN001 0716
2 4 6 8 10 9 7 5 3
ISBN 978-1-78440-807-7

Written by Elizabeth Dale
Illustrated by Paula Bowles

Printed and manufactured in China

My Treasury of
Teddy Tales

igloobooks

Contents

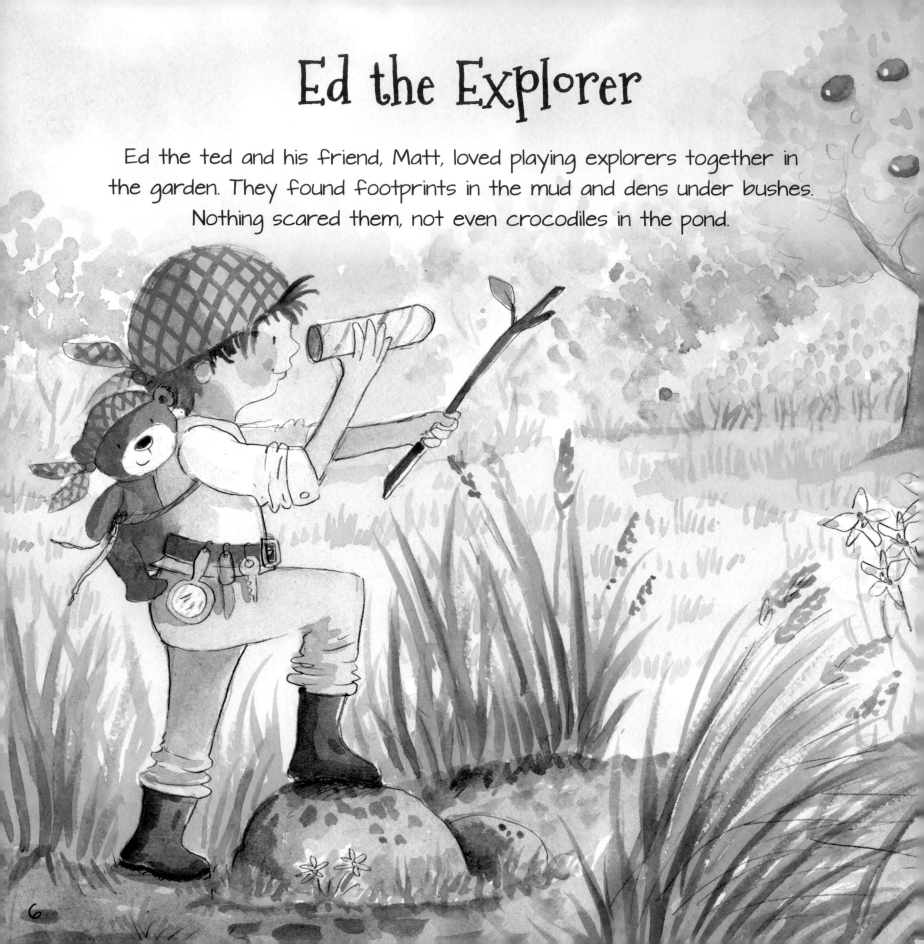

Ed the Explorer

Ed the ted and his friend, Matt, loved playing explorers together in the garden. They found footprints in the mud and dens under bushes. Nothing scared them, not even crocodiles in the pond.

"We are brave explorers off on an exciting adventure!" cried Matt, as he led the way with his stick. "Maybe we will even find a scary monster."

7

Suddenly, Matt saw a shadow behind the shed. "Shh! I think it's a monster."
Just then, Matt's mum called out. "Time for your dinner!" she said.
"Oh, no!" cried Matt. "Ed, you look for the monster and I'll come back later."

Ed was very excited as Matt ran inside. He'd never been on an adventure on his own before. He looked all around him, ready to spot the monster in case it appeared.

As Ed watched and waited, it soon began to get dark. HOOT! Ed jumped.
What was that? He looked all around him and saw something swoop low.
"Maybe it's the monster," said Ted, but it was just an owl.

As it grew darker, Ed heard
snuffling in the long grass.
"I think it's the monster,"
he said, quivering.

The sound was getting
louder and louder,
until suddenly, a rabbit
hopped by.

Ed didn't want to be an explorer all alone in the dark anymore. "I want to go back inside," he said. Just then, he saw a shadow. It grew bigger and came closer and closer. "It's the monster!" he cried.

"There you are, Ed," said a friendly voice. It was Matt.
He picked Ed up and gave him a big cuddle. "Come on," he said.
"That's enough exploring for today."

Teddy Bears' Picnic

All of the teddies were happy today.
Their picnics were always so much fun.
They played pass-the-parcel and Little Brown Ted
jumped up in the air when he won.

They all shared their food, every sandwich and pie
and their delicious, yummy, big cakes.
For drinks, they had cola and all kinds of juice
and truly scrumptious milkshakes.

15

They played hide-and-seek and musical chairs, but Topsy slipped over and fell.

The teddies gave him a big, special prize because he recovered so well.

After they'd played there never had been
more happy or tired-out teds.
Then, singing together, they packed up their things
and tiptoed home to their beds.

17

Little, Lost Teddy

Roly was having a wonderful day in the country with Jack and his family. They rolled down grassy banks and had a lovely picnic. Suddenly, it started to rain and everything was packed up quickly.

In the rush, Roly got left behind. He saw Jack and his family driving
away in a red car. "Maybe he'll come back for me," thought Roly,
but Jack didn't. Hours went by and poor Roly got very wet.

Suddenly, a friendly dog came and sniffed Roly. "Buster, come here!" cried a boy, but Buster wouldn't leave Roly alone. "Hello," said the boy, as he picked Roly up. "I'm Will. I'll look after you."

Will took Roly home and dried him. Then, he asked his dad to help make posters with Roly's picture on. Will was kind and cuddled Roly, but Roly was very sad.

FOUND

The next day, Will took Roly along as he went round sticking the
posters to trees and lamp posts. "You're a lovely teddy bear," said Will.
"Someone will be missing you." Roly missed Jack so much.

22

Days went by, but nobody came for Roly. "Jack has forgotten about me," he sighed. Then, one morning, the doorbell rang. It was Jack! "I saw your poster saying you've found my teddy," he said, as Will handed Roly over. Jack cuddled him. Never was there a happier bear!

The Teddy Show

Teddy was excited, he was putting on a show.
All his friends and family had told him they would go.

He practised some magic tricks. They all were very good.
Except the rabbits didn't appear exactly when they should.

Teddy tried his juggling tricks. He loved them best of all.
He did them standing on one leg and didn't drop one ball.

"I'll do a dance," Teddy said, as he danced and sang a song so sweet.
"The audience will love to see my magnificent dancing feet."

At last it was the big
show night and Teddy
was so thrilled.

He peeped between
the curtains to see
the hall was filled.

28

The show began and it went so well, the audience gave a cheer.
Then, Teddy reached inside his hat and made lots of rabbits appear.

Teddy did some juggling tricks and saved his dance till last.
Then, as he jumped, he tripped and fell and everybody gasped.

The crowd laughed and cheered. "He's funny, too!" they cried.
Instead of bursting into tears, Teddy beamed with pride.

Teeny's Birthday

When Teeny woke one morning, he was such a happy bear.
At last it was his birthday and his friends would soon be there.
He wondered what surprises they had organized last night.
He looked around and then he gasped, for no bear was in sight.

There were no cards beside his bed and no friends to sing a song.
This was supposed to be his day and yet his friends had gone.

He crept downstairs
and looked around, but
found no friends at all...

... not even in the garden...

... or in the lounge or hall.

As Teeny sadly went upstairs, he heard some muffled cries.
He opened the door and gasped and couldn't believe his eyes.
All the bears, in party hats, cheered as they ran out.
Then, they sang 'Happy Birthday', as they waved their arms about.

"Come and dance," they cheered. Then, they cried, "Hip, hip, hooray!
You surely didn't think that we'd forget your special day?"
They gave him gifts and played some games. They had a party tea.
Teeny knew for sure he had the best friends there could be.

Old Grand Ted

Sally's best teddy, Grand Ted, was getting old. More and more he just sat and watched the other teddies having fun. "Grand Ted, swing me round like you used to," said Tweeny.

"I'm too old to swing you round," chuckled Grand Ted. "Show me your handstands instead." Tweeny proudly did ten handstands, but then he toppled over. Luckily, Grand Ted reached over to save him.

RIPPP went Grand Ted's jacket, as he saved Tweeny. All the teddies looked horrified. "Don't worry," said Grand Ted, smiling. "You're an old teddy, but you're still precious," said Tweeny, climbing on Grand Ted's knee.

38

Just as Grand Ted was telling an exciting story, Sally's mummy
came in to tidy the playroom. "Look at you! You're ripped and mucky.
You need a big, bubbly bath," she said, picking up Grand Ted.

First, Sally's mummy ran a warm, bubbly bath for Grand Ted. She even added a rubber duck, too.

Then, she replaced his lost stuffing, mended all his holes and put on his lovely, clean clothes.

The teddies hardly recognized Grand Ted when he returned.
"Hooray!" cried Tweeny. "Just in time for our bedtime story."
"First things first," said Grand Ted and then he swung Tweeny round.
Everyone cheered. Grand Ted was a whole new teddy.

Snuggles' Big Adventure

Leo was very excited. He was going to the Adventureland theme park. "I know I usually take you everywhere with me," Leo told Snuggles, his teddy, "but some of the rides might be really scary, so I'm leaving you at home today."

Snuggles frowned. She didn't want to go on really scary rides, but surely Leo would need her if he was frightened? Leo hugged her goodbye and then put her down on his bed. Whoops! Suddenly, Snuggles fell into Leo's backpack.

43

Leo loved Adventureland. Whoosh! The roundabout spun round and round.

"Whee!" cried Leo.
"This is fun."
Snuggles thought so, too.

The runaway train was very steep and scary. As they whooshed down the tracks, Snuggles peeped out. She loved fast rides and Leo did, too. "I'm flying!" he cried.

The ghost train was even scarier. There were big bats and spooky spiders. Leo was scared and wished Snuggles was there. Snuggles was scared, too. Just then, she poked out her arm.

"Snuggles!" cried Leo. "How did you get into my backpack?"
Snuggles smiled. Leo cuddled her tightly, he was so relieved that
she was there to keep him safe.

Next, Leo and Snuggles went on the tallest roller coaster in Adventureland. Leo had been too scared to go on it before, but with Snuggles to cuddle, he knew he'd be fine. "Wheee!" he cried, as they zoomed down the track.

The rest of the rides were just as fun and they couldn't wait
to come back next time. Their day out at Adventureland had been the
best day, ever, but being together was the best part of all.

Ben the New Teddy

A new bear had come to the playroom one day.
The old toys were worried they'd be thrown away.
The bear had bright eyes and he looked so cute,
in his shiny hat and bright red velvet suit.

"I'm Ben," said the bear. "I'm so glad to be here.
We'll have lots of fun. There's nothing to fear."
But Tiny was scared and ran off to hide.
He opened the toy box and jumped inside.

"What a good idea," said Ben.
"Let's play hide-and-seek."
Then, he counted to ten.
"I promise not to peek."

Ben found Tiny in the
toy box, out of sight.
He tickled him so much
that Tiny giggled in delight.

The toys had fun, as Ben taught them a new song.
Young Tiny danced and giggled, as he sang along.
Ben smiled and asked, "I love it here. Can I stay?"
"Of course you can!" cheered the toys. "Hip, hip, hooray!"

A New Home for Noola

Maisy clutched her best teddy, Noola, as they pulled up outside of her new house. Everything was strange and different and Maisy was worried. "Here we are," said Maisy's mum, smiling. "This is your new home."

"I don't want a new home," Maisy told Noola, as they walked around the strange house. Noola didn't want a new home, either. Maisy hugged her teddy tight. "At least we're together," she said.

"Come and see your new garden," said Maisy's mum. Maisy took Noola outside. The garden was beautiful and there were lots of pretty flowers. There was even a big swing for them to play on. "Whee!" cried Maisy, giggling.

Whenever children came into the shop, Wonky Teddy was disappointed.
They always chose other cuddly toys to take home and some children would
even point at his wonky smile and giggle. "He's so wonky!" they cried.

The other toys in the toy shop felt sorry for Wonky Teddy because they knew how kind and lovely he was. He even told them the best stories when they couldn't sleep at night. He was the perfect teddy.

The toys all cuddled Wonky Teddy each time he wasn't chosen
to go to a new home. Then, one day, Cheeky Monkey had a brilliant idea.
"You just need a little makeover," he said, giggling.

"Your waistcoat is very dusty," said Cheeky Monkey, scratching his head. "I'll wash it for you and make it extra-clean."

Once Cheeky Monkey had finished cleaning Wonky Teddy's jacket, it was a beautiful, bright shade of green and smelt lovely, too.

"You'll have a new home before you know it," said Cuddly Bear, smiling. "But first, your fur needs to be extra-soft and fluffy." Cuddly Bear brushed and brushed and before long, Wonky's fur was the softest he'd ever felt.

As Dolly lovingly tied a big, red bow round his neck, Fairy Bella waved her wand. "Now all you need is a little bit of magic," she said, sprinkling fairy dust over him. Just then, a little girl came in to the toy shop.

"Oh, you are so adorably wonky!" cried the girl, as she picked him up and gave him the biggest cuddle. "You need lots of love and I will give it to you." Wonky Teddy smiled happily. Someone wanted him at long last.

The Teddy Olympics

Tiny Ted jumped up and down, he couldn't wait to start.
The Toy Olympics had begun and he was taking part.
The whistle blew and Tiny started off the race quite well.
Then, everybody ran ahead and Tiny tripped and fell.

68

The rubber-boot-throwing looked such fun, but when Tiny Ted threw his boot in the air, it landed on his head.

He came last in the hopping race and in the high jump, too.

"Never mind," said Tubby Bear. "There's still a prize for you."

Poor Tiny took his lollipop and sat down with his treat.
But then a bee buzzed round his ear in search of something sweet.
Tiny ran this way and that. He got in a terrible muddle.
"Leave me alone!" cried Tiny, as he leapt right over a puddle.

"Hooray!" the teddies yelled and cheered. They couldn't believe their eyes.
For Tiny Ted had leapt so far, he won the long jump prize.
Then, Tiny smiled and took a bow. He had never jumped so far or fast.
To think a little bear like him had won a prize at last!

Grumpy Ted

Grumpy Ted was the grumpiest teddy the other toys had ever met.
When he first came into the toy room Grumpy was scowling and hadn't stopped
since. All the other toys tried their best to cheer him up.

Topsy pulled funny faces and Old Ted did his silly dance, but nothing could turn Grumpy's frown into a smile. "Oh, Grumpy, no one likes a grump," they all said. Grumpy just scowled even more.

One day, when Topsy was reading a story to everyone, Grumpy fell asleep with the grumpiest frown on his face. "We have to stop him being so miserable," said Jessie Cat. "It must be horrible being so unhappy."

"I've got an idea," said Old Ted, opening the dressing-up box.

First, Robot found a sparkly, purple wig.

Then, Topsy found a pair of star-shaped glasses.

Finally, Jessie Cat found a funny jester's hat.

"Why are you all looking at me?" said Grumpy, as the toys led him to a mirror. He stared at his reflection for a moment, Suddenly, he let out a little giggle and then a chuckle, until eventually, he laughed the loudest laugh they'd ever heard. "Laughing is so much fun!" he cried.

From then on, Grumpy Ted was always laughing. "We can't call you Grumpy anymore," said Topsy. "We'll call you Happy Ted, instead." Happy Ted loved his new name, but he loved smiling even more.

Little Bear by the Sea

Little Bear was very excited. It was her first visit to the seaside with Sophia and they were going to have such fun. The sea sparkled and the sand was tickly. Sophia left Little Bear on the beach towel.

"Can we all go for a swim?" Sophia asked her parents.
"We'll go, but you must leave Little Bear here," said Dad. "Bears can't swim."

Little Bear sat and watched Sophia giggle as she played in the splashy waves. Little Bear was glad she was left on the beach. She didn't like getting wet. Just then, two children ran past her, eating ice creams.

PLOP! Something cold landed on Little Bear's nose. She wiped it off with her paw and licked it. Yummy!

Suddenly, she heard a loud squawk. A big seagull swooped down and grabbed her ribbon.

Little Bear was lifted high up into the air. "Wheee! I'm flying!" she cried, but as the seagull soared higher, Little Bear started to feel scared. Suddenly, the friendly seagull let go of her ribbon.

BOING! Little Bear
landed on a bouncy castle.
"This is fun!" she said, giggling,
as she bounced up and down.

Just then, a little girl picked
Little Bear up. "You're so cute,"
she said and then she carried
her along the beach.

The girl took Little Bear on a boat ride. She giggled as the boat bobbed up and down.

Suddenly, a big wave went past and Little Bear fell out of the boat. SPLOSH!

Just then, a dog dashed into the sea and saved Little Bear. He bounded along the beach with her and dropped her...

... back onto her towel! As Little Bear sat happily in the sun, cooling water dripped on to her. It was Sophia back from swimming. "Little Bear!" she cried. "It looks like you went swimming without us," she said, giggling. If only she knew.

The Lonely Teddy

Ned the teddy was very lonely. His owner, Adam, liked playing with cars and always forgot about him. One day, Adam's mum told him to sort through the toys he no longer wanted. Ned was worried. "What if I'm next?" he thought.

Ned recalled the days when Adam was younger. They had so much fun...

... playing on the swings in the park...

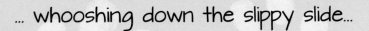
... whooshing down the slippy slide...

... and feeding the cute ducks and swans.

That afternoon, Adam's little sister, Tilly, came rushing in. "This is Lola, my new doll!" she said, beaming with pride. "Isn't she beautiful?" "No," said Adam. "Dolls are silly!" Ned felt sorry for Lola. He thought she looked lovely with her big, friendly smile.

That night, just as Ned was feeling lonelier than ever, he saw a small shadow by the door. It was Lola. "Hello," she said. "Would you like to be my friend?" "Oh, yes please," he said, smiling. Lola and Ned played all night long.

The next day, Adam's mummy came in with a big, black bag.
"It's time to get rid of all the toys you don't play with any more," she said.
Poor Ned froze with fear. Would Adam throw him away?

"If you're throwing toys away, please can I have Ned,?" asked Tilly, running in. Adam agreed and Tilly cuddled Ned and Lola together. The two toys smiled. They would be friends forever and Ned would never be lonely again.

Goodnight, Baby Bear

It was night-time and the stars and moon shone bright.
All the toys and teddy bears were sleeping through the night.
All except for Baby Bear, who tossed and turned and sighed.
"Baby Bear, what is wrong?" his mummy woke and cried.

Baby yawned and rubbed his eyes, then sadly shook his head.
"The dark and shadows scare me," the little teddy said.
"I wish the night would end, so that we could start the day.
Then, I could see my friends and we could laugh and play."

93

"Baby Bear," said Mummy, "come here and stand by me.
We'll look up at the clear night sky and then you'll clearly see,
that the moon and stars shine brightly, specially for me and you.
Until the morning sun comes up, they sparkle all night through."

"Settle down, Baby Bear," said Mummy. "Rest your head,
It's getting late and now it's time to snuggle up in bed.
Have sweet dreams, for now you know there's nothing for you to fear.
When you wake, as always, I'll be waiting for you here."

"We need the dark," said Mum. "It helps us to sleep at night,
but you might feel much happier, with little night-time light."
She hurried off and carried back a light shaped like a star.
Baby smiled, "That's better. Now, I can see just where you are."

Maisy and Noola v
visit Sarah. "You'
your teddy!" cried
"Here, meet

All afternoon, the two girls
played happily with their teddies.
"Would you like to stay for
a sleepover?" asked Sarah.

st then, a little girl popped her head over the fence.
"My name is Sarah. I live next door. Would you like to come round
Maisy smiled. Sarah looked nice and Noola thought so, too.